My Fake Girlfriend
Friends to Lovers Series
by
Reba Bale

My Fake Girlfriend

Friends to Lovers, Volume 5

Reba Bale

Published by Reba Bale, 2022.

MY FAKE GIRLFRIEND

© 2022 by Reba Bale

Cover by Paper or Pixels

This is a work of fiction. Similarities to real people, places, or events are entirely coincidental.

MY FAKE GIRLFRIEND

First edition. July 15, 2022.

Copyright © 2022 Reba Bale.

ISBN: 979-8215148006

Written by Reba Bale.

Also by Reba Bale

Affair Recovery
Share Me: A Cheating Husband's Punishment

Dancing with Strangers
Taken by Surprise: A Billionaire Boss Romance

Friends to Lovers
The Divorcee's First Time: A Hot Friends-to-Lovers Lesbian
Romance
My BFF's Sister
My Rockstar Assistant
My College Crush
My Fake Girlfriend
My Secret Crush

Paying for Tuition

The Billionaire's Assistant
The Babysitter's Ride Home
The Babysitter's First Ménage
The Teaching Assistant's Lesson

Punishing Holidays
Turkey and a Spanking
Shopping and a Spanking

Sharing With Strangers
The Ride of My Life

Spanking Therapy Clinic
The Reluctant Bride's First Spanking
The Reluctant Bride Gets Caught
The Billionaire Gets Punished
The Curvy Reporter Gets Punished

The Divorce Recovery Team
Spanking Justice
A Punishing Workout
A Disciplined Budget

The Marriage Survival Retreat
Finding His Alpha
Watching His Wife
Exploring His Fantasy

The Voyeur Romance Series
Naughty Dinner Date
Naughty Laundry Day
Naughty Camping
Naughty Love Story
Naughty Sunbathing

Toys for Grown-Ups
Ménage a Geek
Financial Punishment

Unlikely Doms
Alpha in a Sweater Vest
Alpha Student
Alpha Yogi

Standalone

Hotel Spanking
Unlikely Doms
Divorce Recovery Team: A Punishment Experiment Collection
Spicing Up My Marriage
It Takes Three
The Christmas Swap
Sinful Desires

Table of Contents

About This Book

The woman she's had a crush on for years needs a fake girlfriend, and Elana is ready to volunteer for the job!

Toya is in a bind. Her little sister is getting married, and her mother is insisting she bring her girlfriend to the wedding. She'd told a little white lie to get her mom off her back, but now it's backfiring. Her mom thinks she's in a committed relationship, so Toya needs to find a pretend girlfriend, and fast.

Elana fell in love with Toya the minute she set eyes on her. Unfortunately, she somehow went right into the friend zone. Elana has been hesitant to rock the boat, especially when they have so many friends in common, but this wedding is a chance for her to finally show Toya how she feels.

Pretending to be a couple and sharing a bed at the destination wedding, things start to heat up. Suddenly things between them aren't so friendly...

Can she convince Toya that she needs more than being a fake girlfriend? She needs forever.

"My Fake Girlfriend" is book five in the "Friends to Lovers" romantic novella series. Each book in the series is a steamy standalone featuring an LGBTQ couple making the leap from friends to lovers and looking for their "happily ever after".

Be sure to check out a free preview of "Spanking Justice: A Middle-Aged Divorcee's First Spanking" at the end of this book!

***

Want a free book? Join my newsletter and receive a free book for signing up. I promise I will only email you when there are new releases or special sales, go to bit.ly/rebabooks and sign up today.

Toya

My phone rang and I rolled my eyes when I saw my mother's name on the screen. I debated sending her to voicemail, but I knew my mom well enough to know that she would just keep bugging me until I picked up. Might as well get it over with. I loved my mother, but she had definite opinions about how I should live my life, and after thirty-five years, it got old.

"Hey Mom."

"Hi Baby, your sister says you never returned your RSVP card for the wedding."

I frowned at the phone. "Why would I RSVP? I'm the freaking maid of honor, she knows I'll be there."

"But what about your guest?"

"What guest?"

Mom sighed like I was a huge disappointment. "Toya, you're not thinking of coming to the wedding alone, are you?"

"I'll be busy doing maid of honor shit, I won't have time to entertain someone else."

"If you don't bring someone, we'll have an uneven number. It'll look weird and mess up the seating chart."

Good lord, she'd heard about bridezillas, but she had no idea her mother would turn into a mother-of-the-bridezilla. Meanwhile her sister, the actual bride, had been completely chill about the whole event. She'd even let Toya pick out her own dress.

"Who exactly am I supposed to bring, Mom?"

"What about your new girlfriend?"

"Wh—," I stopped myself from asking "what girlfriend?" just in the nick of time.

Thinking fast, I said, "Why would I bring her? We've only been dating for a few months."

I'd nearly forgotten that a few weeks ago I'd told my mother I was dating someone so she would stop giving me her "you're going to die alone" speech.

"Are you embarrassed of your family?" Mom asked in her long-suffering tone. "Is that why you never want to introduce your girlfriends to us? You know we've always supported your being a lesbian, unlike a lot of terrible parents."

I rolled my eyes so hard I think I caught a glimpse of my own brain. It was true though, my parents had been extremely chill when I came out to them. It probably helped that they suspected I was a lesbian since I was a little kid, long before I even understood what it meant.

"Fine Mom, I'll see if my girlfriend will come, but I can't guarantee anything on such short notice."

"What did you say her name was again?" Mom asked.

I hadn't said her name before, I was sure of that. Probably because I'd made the whole thing up. Thinking fast, I said the first name that popped into my head.

"Elana."

Elana

I walked up to the table of women in the corner of the restaurant and smiled. It had been a rough day but just seeing my friends waiting for me improved my mood dramatically.

I'd moved to Seattle a while back and had been pretty damn lonely until I met my friend Jewel about six months ago. We'd met at the gym and instantly clicked, becoming fast friends.

Jewel and her partner Alice had brought me into the fold, inviting me to their monthly "friend dinners" which included a great group of strong and smart lesbian women. When I joined the group I'd met Miranda and Elizabeth, who were living together, and Jennifer and Susan, who were married. Our friend Christine also came out with us when she wasn't on tour with her rockstar girlfriend, Lila.

And then there was Toya. She and I were the only single ones in the group, and as much as I might hope that would change, I knew it wasn't possible. I'd fallen for Toya the minute I saw her. It was love at first sight, like in one of those crazy old movies.

She was a tall, beautiful black woman with light caramel skin, large brown eyes, and curly dark hair with golden highlights. She had a banging body, fit but curvy, with a narrow waist, strong thighs, generous hips, and the best pair of tits I'd ever seen. And I'd seen plenty, thank you very much.

I might be a short, curvy Mexican girl, but I did okay for myself dating-wise. Except no one excited me like Toya. The first time our eyes met I'd fallen in love with her, but she'd put me firmly in the friend zone. In the early days I'd tried to flirt with her, but receiving no encouragement, I settled for just being her friend. I knew that no amount of wishing could make someone attracted to you if you weren't their type. I'd heard from other friends that Toya had a penchant for tall, thin beauties.

"Ah, there she is," Elizabeth called. "We were just talking about taking a group trip to Sagebrush, the retreat center where Miranda and I found each other again."

She sent her partner a sappy smile before adding, "There's a lesbian only weekend at the end of summer."

"Sounds fun," I said, sitting in the open chair between Toya and Jewel. "I'm in."

I subtly inhaled the orange scented fragrance that Toya wore. I didn't know if it was lotion or cologne or what, but she always smelled citrusy. I loved it.

Toya leaned in so she could whisper in my ear. "Hey, after we're done here, can I give you a ride home? You took the bus, right?"

I nodded. I wasn't much for driving if I didn't have to. Plus, parking was a nightmare in this city and if there was one thing I hated, it was driving around looking for a parking spot.

Toya continued, "There's something I want to talk to you about."

"Sure," I said, feigning casual.

This was strange. Toya and I had never spent any time alone before. I couldn't imagine what she had to talk to me about that she couldn't say in front of our friends. I spent the rest of our group dinner wondering what Toya had on her mind that involved me. I didn't have to wait long. We'd scarcely gotten in the car when Toya turned to face me.

"I need a favor," she said. "A huge favor. But I won't be mad if you say no. I mean, you probably won't feel comfortable, and I get that, I totally do. It's just that, I'm only asking because I did something ridiculous and now I'm really in a bind."

I frowned. It wasn't like Toya to babble like this.

"What do you need?" I asked her. "A kidney or something?"

Toya laughed, but it was humorless.

"I need you to pretend to be my girlfriend."

"What?" My voice raised several octaves higher than it usually was.

Toya looked embarrassed. "Okay, I'm going to tell you something but please don't tell the others, it makes me look really bad."

I crossed my fingers over my heart. "I promise."

"My mom has been bugging me about getting a girlfriend and I was getting super annoyed about it so finally I told her I was seeing someone. I know it's ridiculous for a grown woman to lie to her mom like that, but I just wanted her to get off my back for a while. That woman is like a dog with a bone when she's on a mission. I'd almost forgotten about it until she informed me that she wanted me to bring my girlfriend to my sister's wedding in a couple of weeks."

She paused and met my eyes in a way that made my heart beat faster.

"I, um, I told her that you were my girlfriend."

"What?" That high-pitched voice was back.

"She asked me for a name, and yours was the first one that popped into my head. Plus, she's met all the other girls in our group, so I knew she wouldn't believe I was dating one of them. So anyway, now my mom thinks you're my girlfriend."

"So, you're asking me to what...go to your sister's wedding with you?"

Toya nodded. "Yeah, it's this whole weekend thing down in Bend. If you can get off work, we would drive down on Thursday, do the rehearsal on Friday, the wedding is on Saturday, then we'd come back on Sunday."

She grasped my hand, and I felt a frisson of electricity. My heart started pounding again.

"I know it's a lot to ask, but... can you at least think about it? You've never been to Bend, right? When we're not doing wedding shit we can go see the sights. I'll pay for everything."

"We would have to get our stories straight before I meet your family."

Toya looked hopeful. "Yes, I figured we could talk about all that on the way down to Bend. It's like a six hour drive, seven if the traffic on I-5 is bad."

I had a bad feeling that this trip would only make me more obsessed with this woman who just saw me as a friend. On the other hand, Toya wasn't one to ask people for favors. I couldn't tell her no, even if I wanted to. I liked her too much.

Then again, I knew very well what it was like to have a mother who was a pain in the ass. I had a feeling that if I were in a similar situation, I might be tempted to lie to get my mother off my back too.

I studied Toya's hopeful face for a long moment and came to a decision.

"Okay, I'll do it."

Toya

As we drove out of Seattle, I couldn't believe my luck. Elana agreeing to come to the wedding with me was the solution to several of my problems. It was so cool of her to agree to my crazy scheme.

I glanced at her out of the corner of my eye. She was a beautiful woman, with long dark hair and light brown skin that hinted at her mixed race. I knew her dad was white, and her mother was Mexican. She was several inches shorter than me, with full curves, huge almond-shaped brown eyes, and the sweetest smile I'd ever seen.

Although we'd been friends for a minute now, I didn't really know her that well. We usually interacted as part of the larger group, and I'd never really spent any time alone with her. I wasn't sure why that was, but I was looking forward to getting to know her better now.

I looked at her again and caught a whiff of a light floral fragrance that she wore. She really was pretty. When I first met Elana I'd just gone through a horrible break-up and dating was the last thing on my mind. Now we'd been around each other for a long time and I really didn't notice her as a woman. I wondered if I met her now if I would have asked her out.

We'd been quiet for a while before Elana broke the silence.

"Let's talk about our backstory," she said. "Like, how did we meet and when did we get together?"

"I think it's best if we stick as close to the truth as possible," I replied. "We'll say that Jewel brought you to our monthly get-together, and we met each other there about six months ago, which is all true."

"Did we start dating right away?" Elana asked.

I sent her a teasing smirk.

"I didn't want someone else to swoop in, so I got your number that first night and asked you out the next morning."

Elana bit her lip for a second, as if I'd hurt her feelings. I replayed my words in my head, puzzled, but before I could ask about it, she spoke up again.

"Our first date was at Mazzotti's," she said, referencing a nice restaurant in downtown Seattle where our group of friends often met for dinner. "We bonded over our love of Italian food and hiking."

"Oh yeah, I forgot that you're a big hiker too. It's weird that we never went hiking together."

She made a non-committal sound but didn't respond.

"Did we get serious right away?" she asked instead.

I shook my head.

"No, we are definitely a slow-burn kind of couple, especially because it took me a while to get over my last relationship. But you were patient."

"What was your last relationship?" she asked curiously, shifting in her seat to get a better look at me.

"I was dating this woman Tonya," I started.

"Oh my gosh," she snort-laughed. "Toya and Tonya? That's too cute."

I shook my head. "Please, I heard that all the time. Anyway. We dated for like a year and I thought we were getting serious, until I caught her with another woman."

Elana gasped. "You caught them in bed together?"

"They were just kissing, but obviously that was enough for me. I don't stand for cheaters, even though I somehow wind up dating them pretty often."

"So, we started dating and you were a little skittish, but then one thing led to another and...we fell in love?"

"Yep," I said, my mind suddenly going to the "one thing led to another comment" with a visual of me kissing Elana. And maybe more...

Stop it Toya, I chastised myself. *She's your friend, doing you a huge favor. You don't need to be drooling all over her.*

The rest of the trip passed more quickly than I would have expected. After we ironed out the details of our fake relationship, we fell into an easy conversation, punctuated by periods of comfortable silence. It was nice. I hadn't realized how easy it was to talk to Elana. She had a quick wit and was an entertaining storyteller, but she also was skilled at getting others to talk.

We drove down to the Great Bend Resort, where my sister's wedding was happening. The area was beautiful, with ancient trees, wildflowers, and mountains in the near distance. It felt like we were a million miles away from the city up here. I loved it.

I parked my SUV in the lot, and we grabbed our bags, heading to the reception desk to check in. We were waylaid by my mother and sister the second we entered the door. Clearly they had been waiting for us.

"Toya! You're here!"

My sister Tina threw herself into my arms, giving me a tight hug. I laughed and hugged her back.

"Of course I'm here, you doofus. I wasn't going to miss your wedding. This is my one chance to be a maid of honor."

"You must be Elana," my mother said from my other side. "I'm so glad to finally meet you. Toya's been so secretive about you."

She pulled Elana into a hug, and Tina and I rolled our eyes at each other behind our mother's back. I moved over to pull Elana away from my mother, tucking her under my arm. She fit perfectly there with her soft curves pressed against my leaner body.

"I wanted to keep her all to myself for a while," I said, giving her a slight squeeze.

Elana wrapped her arm around my waist, pulling us closer. It was nice. Comfortable. I ignored the tingly feeling that happened everywhere we touched.

"Elana, this is my sister Tina."

Elana reached out to shake my sister's hand.

"Nice to meet you. Congratulations on your wedding."

"Thank you. And nice to meet you too, Elana."

Mom handed us a little envelope with two key cards. "Here are two keys for your room. I checked you in already. Dad and I took care of paying."

"Wow, Mom, that's very nice of you guys. Thank you." I gestured towards the elevator. "I think Elana and I would like a nice quiet evening tonight, if that's okay with you. I know we're both tired after such a long trip."

"Of course Toya," my sister responded immediately. "Damon and I were going to do the same," she said, referring to her fiancé.

"I'll see you in the morning for our salon appointment."

She sent a friendly smile to Elana.

"We'd like you to come too Elana. We're getting mani-pedis."

"Well..."

"Please. I insist."

Elana shook her head. "Great. Thank you. I'd love to."

I squeezed Elana's shoulder again. "Come on, babe. Let's go rest a bit before dinner."

Elana

I followed Toya up to our room. The resort was really nice, decorated in subtle earth tones. There was a ginormous fireplace in the lobby, made entirely out of river rocks, and large windows looked out over the nearby river. It was both rustic and elegant. I loved it.

"Here we are," Toya said, opening the door to our room.

I followed her in, looking around. It was a nice room. Like the common area, the room was decorated in earth colors. The walls were a warm brown color, decorated with pictures of local attractions, while the carpet was forest green. A matching green couch sat to one side, facing a dark wood coffee table and a large TV. I turned my head and my eyes zeroed in on the bed. The one bed.

"There's only one bed," I pointed out unnecessarily.

Toya nodded. "Uh, yeah. Let me call downstairs and see if we can switch to a room with two doubles."

I went to the bathroom to pee, admiring the marble countertops and large jacuzzi tub. After taking care of my bio needs, I washed my hands and face. When I came back out into the room, Toya was sitting on the edge of the king-sized bed looking sheepish.

"There's no other rooms available," she told me. "They said they're totally booked up this weekend. I guess we'll have to share."

She patted the pristine white comforter. "At least it's a big bed."

My throat was suddenly dry. It had been hard enough being so close to her in the car for so many hours. How was I supposed to sleep in the same bed as the woman who'd had a starring role in my dirtiest dreams over the last six months? Damn, I wasn't expecting this.

"Okay," I said because, really, what else could I say? Suddenly my stomach growled, loudly. We both laughed.

"I've got an idea," Toya said. "But tell me if it's too boring or you want to do something else. It's totally fine."

I nodded.

"How about if we order pizza and beer and just watch a movie?" She said it quickly, like she was embarrassed. "I gotta admit, I'm wiped from that long drive."

It had taken us over seven hours to get there, between traffic and stopping for gas and bathroom breaks. Toya wasn't the only one who was exhausted.

"That sounds perfect. Honestly, I'm kind of a homebody most of the time. I never really went anywhere until Jewel adopted me."

She laughed. "I don't go out that much either. I did the whole go-go-go thing when I was in my twenties but now at this age? I just like to be comfortable and get my rest, even if that makes me boring."

"I'm more than happy to be boring with you."

For a boring night, it was really fun. Toya ran out to get us some beer and brownies while I ordered the pizza. When the food arrived, we settled on the small couch in our room, eating our weight in pizza and watching two movies back to back. By the time we were done, I was ready for bed.

I changed into sleep shorts and a tank top while Toya got ready for bed in the bathroom, then I took my turn getting ready for bed. While I brushed my teeth I wondered if this bathroom was larger than my living room. I think it was. When I returned she was already in bed, leaning against the headboard reading. The room was lit only by the lamps on the bedside table, giving it kind of a romantic glow.

Toya looked up with a smile.

"I didn't know you wear glasses. You look so cute."

I felt my face heat at the compliment.

"I prefer contacts, but I can't wear them at night," I explained unnecessarily.

I slipped under the thin blanket, flipping off the light on my side of the bed before settling on my side, knees bent, facing away from Toya.

"Hey Elana?" Toya's voice was soft and tentative.

"Yeah?"

"Thanks for being so cool about all this. I really owe you for helping me out."

"You don't owe me a thing," I responded.

"I was thinking tomorrow we could go to Smith Rock. Other than our morning mani-pedi appointments, we don't have to be anywhere until the rehearsal at six."

I flipped on my back and turned my head to face her. "Really? That would be awesome."

Smith Rock was a challenging but popular place to hike near Bend, and I'd been hoping that we could get over there this weekend. The views were supposed to be incredible. I know that with all the wedding activities we probably wouldn't have too much time for sightseeing, so I was grateful that she figured out a way for us to at least get some hiking in.

Toya reached over and rubbed my arm with her hand. "Good night."

"Good night."

I turned over and to my surprise, fell asleep quickly and slept soundly. The next time I opened my eyes the sun was streaming in through the windows, bathing the room in a bright light.

I felt something shift behind me and realized that during the night I'd moved more towards the center of the bed from where I started. Toya was spooning me, her arm over my waist.

I wish I could wake up like this every day, I thought to myself.

Toya startled, as if I'd spoken aloud.

"Oops, sorry about that," she laughed as she pulled away. "I guess Sleeping Toya gets a little handsy."

I bit my lip, immediately feeling the absence of her soft body behind me. I'd been telling myself that it was just a crush, but the truth was that I was hopelessly in love with my friend. I only hoped to God I was going to be able to get through this weekend without making a fool of myself.

Toya

As I brushed my teeth, I chastised myself for snuggling up against Elana like that. She probably thought I was a total weirdo. In my defense, I'd been sleeping when I wrapped myself around her. I'd been as surprised as she probably was when I woke up to find her curvy ass pressing against my belly.

I spat out my toothpaste and started my skincare routine. As I slathered moisturizer on my skin, I wondered why I was suddenly so attracted to Elana. It was like I looked at her in the car and a switch flipped inside of me. Suddenly I was seeing my friend in a new light. When I woke up snuggled against her this morning, I'd felt a sensation of rightness. A feeling like I wanted to wake up just like this, every day for the rest of my life.

The problem was, I wasn't sure how she felt about me. I shook my head, telling myself to stop being so damn ridiculous. I hadn't dated in quite a while. Maybe this wasn't about Elana at all, maybe I was just horny.

Elana and I headed downstairs, stopping in the cute little coffee shop to grab coffee and pastries. It was a warm morning, so we sat out on the deck, gazing out on the mountains in the distance.

"This is a nice place," Elana said. "We'll have to come out here again sometime. Um, I mean I'll have to come out here again."

"Yeah it's awesome," I responded. "I just love this area. Every time I come I tell myself to visit more often."

I heard laughter and looked up to see my mom, my sister, and her two best friends coming towards us. I was going to be the maid of honor in the wedding, and Tina's two friends were the bridesmaids. I was glad she hadn't gone overboard with some gigantic wedding party.

"Good morning! Happy Wedding Eve baby sister," I called.

Tina gave me a happy smile. My sister was so in love with her fiancé it was almost painful to watch. Damon was perfect for her. They'd broken up for a while over some misunderstanding, but their relationship was stronger than ever after they worked it all out. I was happy for her. Truly. If I felt a slight twinge of jealousy that I didn't have what she had, well, that was perfectly normal, right?

"You ready for some salon time?" my sister asked.

"Yep." I stood up, gathering our trash. "You ready Elana?"

"Yes."

We spent the next two hours sipping mimosas as we got our fingernails and toenails shaped and painted. I wasn't usually a manicure kind of girl – I worked as a carpenter, so my nails always looked like shit – but I had to admit it was fun to get pampered. Plus, my mother assured me that these fancy gel manicures would last much longer than a regular one.

It looked like Elana was having fun too. She was more of a girly girl than I was, and she'd clicked with my mom and sister right away. The three of them were laughing away like they were old friends.

Mom came to sit next to me, and nodded at Elana, who was getting the final touches on her fingernails. Elana had chosen a deep purple polish that contrasted with her light brown skin, while I'd gone with a dusty rose that would match my dress for the wedding.

"You picked a good one this time," Mom said, giving me a side hug. "Elana is awesome."

I glanced at my friend, noticing how the sun was bringing out the red highlights in her dark brown hair. My heart thumped painfully against my sternum.

"Yeah. She is a good one."

When we finished up at the salon, we grabbed a quick lunch with the rest of the bridal party. Then Elana and I headed back to the room to change clothes for our hiking trip. We put on shorts, tank tops, and hiking boots, ready to hit the trail.

We made the thirty minute drive to Smith Rock, parking in the lot. I was surprised how crowded it was. I guessed this really was a popular place.

Grabbing our portable water bottles and sunglasses, we stopped to take a selfie of the two of us with the rock formations in the background. We followed the map to our trail for the day. Last night we'd chosen one of the scenic trails that was just long enough to give us a good view and a good workout, but not totally wipe us out for the rehearsal dinner.

It was a warm day, but it was a dry heat, so it was bearable. Despite the crowded parking lot, we didn't see too many other people on the trail, which I appreciated. We hiked up steadily to the overlook that would be our turning around point, chatting about anything and everything. It was breathtakingly beautiful, and we stopped several times to take pictures and just enjoy nature's majesty as we made our way up to the scenic overlook at the top of this trail.

When we reached our turnaround point we stopped for a while, drinking and stretching a bit before making our way back down.

"Damn, I'm in good shape but I can feel my quads screaming from all this climbing," I told Elana.

"You're working different muscles than you usually do though," she reminded me.

"Maybe you can massage my legs for me later," I joked.

Elana rolled her eyes but didn't respond. Meanwhile, I was fantasizing about us trading dirty massages. Damn it, what was wrong with me?

Elana made a little squeak as her foot slipped on some loose rock. She started to pitch forward, but I grabbed her arm, pulling her back against me. I wrapped my arm around her waist to help her regain her balance.

"Are you okay?" I asked.

"Yeah," she said breathlessly.

She turned around to face me, but I kept my arm on her waist, keeping her near me under the guise of stabilizing her. We were close now, close enough that all I had to do was lean forward a couple of inches and I could close the distance between us and kiss her. I was having a hard time remembering why that would be a bad idea.

The air between us seemed to shimmer. Elana's eyes darted down to my lips, and I licked them without intending to. I saw a flash of heat on her face and wondered if I was the only one feeling this budding attraction between us.

Before I could say anything, she stepped back with a laugh that sounded forced. "Thanks for saving me from wiping out."

She started hiking again, her pace determined.

"I think we're almost to the bottom."

Even that innocent comment was enough to fan my rising libido. I dropped my eyes to her ass, appreciating the way her generous globes flexed as she hiked. I was so fucked.

Elana

When we got back to the hotel, Toya and I took turns taking showers, then got dressed for the wedding rehearsal. I didn't need to be there since I wasn't in the wedding party, but I decided to tag along anyway rather than just meeting them for dinner.

As we exited the elevator into the lobby, Toya grabbed my hand, threading her fingers through mine. She leaned down and whispered in my ear.

"Gotta keep up appearances."

I squeezed her hand in response. We walked through the lobby and outside towards the building where the wedding would take place.

Toya moved to the front of the chapel to get instructions from the wedding coordinator while I settled into a pew in the back of the adorable wedding space. It was a peaceful spot. It looked like something out of a fairy tale with its dark wood pews, stained glass windows, and fairy lights. I could see why this place was popular for weddings. Just the pictures alone would be incredible.

As the wedding party practiced for the big day, I replayed my hiking trip with Toya. My God, when I'd tripped and she caught me I'd been so embarrassed, at least until I turned around. Toya's arm had been on my waist, our faces mere inches away. Her eyes had darkened, and I'd had the strangest feeling like she was going to kiss me. But of course that was ridiculous; she only saw me as a friend.

I'd stared at her, standing there in the sun with the mountain in the background, and had reminded myself that I needed to be careful. I didn't want to make things awkward between us or do anything that would impact our larger friend group. I liked those women too much to lose them as friends. Then Toya had licked her lips and I damn near came on the spot. It had taken every ounce of will power I had to pull away and start walking again before I'd done something stupid like kiss my fake girlfriend.

Speaking of fake girlfriends, Toya's mom came to sit next to me. She was a friendly woman, a little plump, with an unlined brown face, almond shaped eyes, and hair that was straightened into a sedate bob.

"Did you girls have fun hiking?" Mrs. Hamilton asked.

"Yes, it was beautiful."

I rubbed my stomach.

"Plus, we burned a ton of calories so I'm planning on eating whatever I want tonight."

Mrs. Hamilton laughed. "Please girl, you don't have anything to worry about. Your curves are beautiful."

I resisted the urge to pull her into a hug and start sobbing on her shoulder. My own mother was always telling me that I needed to lose weight. Mom was naturally tall and thin and didn't seem to understand that my body would be short and curvy no matter how much I dieted. It had taken me years to build up enough self-esteem to be comfortable in my own body.

"Are you excited about the wedding?" I asked Toya's mom.

Mrs. Hamilton nodded.

"It's going to be beautiful. Tina and Damon are so happy, so in love. It's been a journey for them, but I'm glad they're finally getting their happily ever after."

Her sharp eyes turned to mine.

"You and my daughter seem very much in love. Maybe we'll have another wedding in the family soon?" she asked pointedly.

Just then Toya came up to us. I looked around, noting that the rehearsal was finished, and the bridal party was dispersing.

"Mom, stop harassing my girlfriend," Toya chided.

I ignored the flash of warmth I got every time she called me her girlfriend. I reminded myself once again that it wasn't real. Toya just saw me as a friend, and I was setting myself up for heartbreak thinking otherwise.

"We've only been dating six months," Toya told her mother. "It's a little early to be talking about weddings."

Mrs. Hamilton scoffed. "Please, I knew within a week of meeting your father that he was the man I was going to marry. And I was right."

"We've got time, Mom."

"Just don't wait too long. There's no way Tina is going to give me as many grandchildren as I want all by herself."

A vision of Toya and I staring down at a sweet little baby ran through my mind before I pushed it away.

"Are you hungry?" Toya asked me.

"Ravenous."

"Let's head on over to the restaurant then, the others will be there soon."

She took my hand and pulled me to standing, then wrapped her arms around my waist, pulling me close. Our eyes met and held as everything around us came to a standstill. I swayed closer, while maintaining eye contact. Our reverie was broken by Toya's sister.

"Aww, you two are so damn cute," Tina said.

We stepped apart, and I realized that I was breathing heavily. Toya ran her hand down my arm to thread her fingers through mine again and I shivered at the contact.

"Time for grub."

As we walked out of the chapel to head to dinner a voice chanted in my head on repeat.

Protect yourself. Protect yourself.

Toya

"Kiss. Kiss."

I clinked my fork against my glass and my sister rolled her eyes.

"That's for the wedding, not the rehearsal," Tina protested.

My future brother-in-law sent me a big smile.

"I think she's right baby, we should practice every part of the event, just to make sure we've got it down for tomorrow."

Damon wrapped his arm around Tina and laid a kiss on her lips that was so hot even I got hot and bothered. Speaking of hot and bothered, the more time I spent with Elana this weekend, the more attraction I felt for her. It was all I could think about. Somehow I'd developed some kind of Elana obsession. It was like I could feel where she was at all times, and my body mourned when she wasn't close to me.

I was confused by how quickly things seemed to have changed between us. I had a feeling that I wasn't alone in this attraction, but I couldn't tell for sure. Unlike me, who wore my heart on her sleeve, Elana was pretty hard to read.

Dinner went by quickly, and then we all decided to hit one of the bars at the resort. My parents and Damon's parents begged off, leaving just the wedding party and their plus-ones. We snagged a couple of tables on one side of the bar, basically taking over that side between all of us.

Elana and I both ordered a local IPA, then a little while later someone ordered us all tequila shots for our second round. We all drank a toast to the happy couple, throwing back the shots. I wasn't one to drink that much, so by the time the second round of shots came by, I was feeling damn happy. Not drunk, just that place where your inhibitions are starting to drop.

I wrapped my arm around Elana's shoulders, mimicking some of the other couples. I saw her glance at me out of the corner of her eye, but her face was otherwise emotionless.

The third round of shots came, and it made me bold. I wanted to know if Elana was as affected by me as I was by her. I'd had just enough alcohol to take away any hesitation I would have had if I was completely sober. I shifted my chair even closer to her and deciding to be bold, I laid my hand on her knee. She was wearing a knee-length skirt that had shifted up a bit when she sat down, so my hand landed on bare flesh. I sensed, rather than heard, her sharp intake of breath.

After a few minutes I slid my hand up a few inches, gripping her strong thigh and caressing her skin with my thumb. Her skin was smooth as silk beneath my fingers. Tentatively, I slid my hand up higher. Elana's face showed no emotion, but she wasn't slapping my hand away, so I kept going. To my surprise and excitement, she widened her legs, just enough for me to slip my hand between them.

My fingers continued slowly traveling up until they met the fabric of her panties. Fabric that was damp with arousal. I pressed my fingers against her core, rubbing slightly. Elana jumped out of her chair like she'd sat on a pin cushion, shoving her chair back loudly. My hand dropped and everyone at the table turned to look at her, no doubt wondering why she stood up so abruptly.

"Please excuse us," she said calmly.

She reached down and grabbed my hand, dragging me out of the restaurant behind her. For such a little thing, she was pretty strong. As she towed me behind her, I wondered if she was mad at me for getting fresh with her. Then I remembered those damp panties.

The minute we got outside, Elana swung me around so that my back was against the building. Without a word, she pressed me between her body and the rough surface of the wall with her torso and reached up and grabbed the back of my head, drawing my head down to where she could reach. Okay then, definitely not mad at me.

The minute our lips touched, everything else faded away. I wrapped my arms around her shoulders, pulling her closer, but otherwise was content to let her lead.

Elana nipped my lower lip, demanding entrance. The instant my mouth opened, her tongue swooped in, sliding along mine and exploring the recesses of my mouth. She moaned, deepening the kiss even more.

I felt a rush of arousal hit me like a tsunami and suddenly Elana wasn't the only one with damp panties.

I was no stranger to first kisses. I'd dated a lot of women in my thirty-five years but this, this felt like something more. Something life changing. I knew instinctively that no other kiss would come close to this one. This woman was it for me. I don't know how I never realized it before, but my eyes were opened now.

Every inch of the front of our bodies pressed against each other as the kiss went on and on. I could feel my clit throbbing in time with my heartbeat, and I rolled my hips against hers, seeking friction. Elana widened her stance, straddling one of my thighs, and I bent my knees slightly to line up with her better as we ground against each other.

When she finally pulled away, both of us were gasping for breath. Elana looked a bit shell shocked and a lot aroused. I could see her nipples poking through the fabric of her shirt like little headlights. I didn't need to look down to know I had the same thing going on.

I could feel her watching me, her eyes appraising. Finally, she whispered, "I'm sorry. I shouldn't have done that."

"I'm not sorry at all," I replied. "That was hot as hell."

Her eyes widened.

"Besides, I started it by feeling you up in the bar."

"Well, that's true." She laughed, lightening the mood.

"So, what happens now?" she asked.

Her gaze was suddenly vulnerable. In that moment I knew without a doubt that she felt this too. Maybe it was a mistake, but I'd never felt this strongly about anyone before, never been kissed like that before. I wanted more. Even if we crashed and burned, I wanted to give myself the gift of this weekend with Elana. And if things went well, hopefully my fake girlfriend would be my real girlfriend by the end of the weekend.

I lifted my hand and cupped my palm against her cheek. She closed her eyes, pressing against my palm, but her eyes flew open at my response.

"Now we're going back to the room and I'm going to fuck you senseless."

I pushed away from the wall and started walking towards the door leading towards the main lobby, stopping when I realized that Elana was still standing in the same place, staring at the wall. I hoped she wasn't changing her mind.

"You coming?" I called, holding out a hand.

She startled, as if I'd pulled her out of a reverie. When she turned, her smile was so radiant that I lost my breath.

"I'm coming all right," she said as she strode over to take my hand. "And you will be too. Soon."

Elana

Toya and I were silent as we made our way through the lobby and into the elevator. I was almost afraid to speak, not wanting to break the spell of whatever was happening between us.

When she'd slipped her hand between my legs at the restaurant, I'd almost died. Or come. Or come and then died. I'd dragged her out of the restaurant intending to ask her what game she was playing, but somehow I wound up kissing her instead. My God, that kiss. It was even better than I'd imagined it would be, and believe me, I'd imagined it quite a lot over the last six months.

We walked hand in hand to our room. Toya scanned the key card, pushing the door open. Without a word, she started dragging me towards the giant bed in the center of the room. She unbuttoned her blouse and tossed it aside, standing before me in just a lacy bra that did nothing to hide her generous breasts. Her body was lean and fit from the physical labor she did as a carpenter, but it was still soft and womanly. It was perfect. She was perfect.

"How drunk are you?" I asked.

My voice sounded soft and needy, but I didn't want to move forward if she was too drunk to consent. The last thing I wanted was for her to have regrets in the morning.

"Buzzed, not drunk," she replied. "I know exactly what I'm doing. I. Want. You."

As she spoke, she unclasped her bra. Her large breasts bounced as they escaped their bondage, and I inhaled sharply. Without conscious thought, I reached out and circled one areola with my finger. Toya pressed herself closer and I couldn't resist lowering my head to get a taste. I sucked one brown nipple into my mouth, gliding my tongue around the tip while adding suction. With my hand I pulled on her other nipple, then pinched it lightly.

Toya moaned and slid her fingers into my hair as I switched sides to give the other breast some attention. After a few minutes I pulled back and gave her a smile.

"Your tits are a work of art."

"How about you show me yours?" she asked silkily.

I pulled my blouse over my head, tossing it in the direction of my suitcase, then removed my bra. Toya stared at me like I was the best thing she'd ever seen. At this point in my life, I was pretty comfortable in my own skin, but even still, the way she was looking at me was doing great things for my ego.

"Wow," she whispered. "Elana. You're so beautiful."

Toya stepped closer, pressing our bodies against each other, and lowered her lips to give me a kiss. She had a few inches on me, so her breasts pressed against my shoulders while mine pressed against the top of her stomach. Even still, it felt incredible.

I made a little moaning sound in the back of my throat and reached around to find the zipper on her skirt. I broke away from the kiss long enough to shove her skirt and panties down past her knees, then came back for another scorching kiss.

"On the bed," I ordered when we finally broke apart. "Ass right on the edge."

Toya gave me a long look, then complied. She sat at the edge of the bed with her feet on the floor. She leaned back on her elbows, watching as I lowered myself to my knees and scooched closer to her. With a hand on each knee, I spread her legs apart, baring her pussy to my gaze. It was neatly groomed, and I could see the moisture glistening along the pinkish brown lips.

Slowly I lowered my head, licking along the outside of her slit a few times. I slid my hands up to her thighs, spreading her legs more, and slid my tongue in between the lips of her pussy. I began running my tongue up and down her slit as Toya started wiggling beneath my hands, making needy sounds that just ramped up my arousal.

"Please," she gasped. "Please."

Instinctively knowing what she wanted, I zeroed in on her clit. I tapped it with my tongue a few times, then traced the edges, swirling my tongue around the swollen bud of nerves. Meanwhile, I ran my pointer finger through her moisture and slid it into her tight channel.

"Oh God," Toya wailed. "Elana!"

Her inner walls fluttered against my finger as I began pumping in and out of her while still teasing her clit with the tip of my tongue. Toya's hand came to my head, her fingers gripping my hair almost painfully as she pulled me in tighter, trying to encourage me to add pressure to her clit.

I sucked her clit in between my lips, lightly biting down. Meanwhile I slipped a second finger into her channel, bending my fingers inside her as I searched for that rough patch of tissue that marked her G-spot. I knew when I found it because Toya's hips lifted sharply. I kept my attention divided between the clit and the G-spot, stroking and circling harder and faster until her orgasm hit her. Her entire body spasmed, inside and out, as Toya came with another long wail.

I kept up my motions until she finally collapsed on the bed, panting heavily. Pulling away, I lowered myself to sit on my heels, watching her. She was beautiful, her face pure pleasure.

"I'm dead," she moaned softly. "You killed me, Elana."

I laughed.

"You look alive to me."

She lifted herself onto her elbows to look at me.

"I promise to reciprocate, but damn girl, I'm gonna need a few minutes to recover."

When she collapsed down on the bed again, I shifted to standing. Realizing I was still dressed from the waist down, I kicked off my shoes and removed my skirt and my sopping wet panties. When I turned around, Toya was lifted back on her elbows once more, watching me with a look reminiscent of a lion looking at a gazelle.

"I think I'm recovered now."

Toya

My heart rate finally slowed down from that incredible orgasm Elana had just given me. Who knew my friend was so talented with her tongue? And her fingers? That orgasm was so intense I thought I would black out for a minute.

I scooched myself farther up the bed, then patted the comforter next to me.

"How about you come up here with me, baby?"

I unashamedly checked her out as she walked over to the bed and stretched out next to me. Elana was all soft curves. I rolled to my knees and moved to straddle her thighs before lowering my upper body onto hers. I cupped her face between my hands and kissed her deeply, tasting myself in her mouth. It was hot as hell. She ran her hands up and down my back and shoulders as our tongues tangled.

When we were out of breath I broke away and slid down to worship her breasts. They were way more than a handful, shaped like tear drops with dark red nipples and large areolas. I lowered my mouth to get a taste.

"Ahhh..."

Elana's back arched, bringing her closer to my mouth. I squeezed her breasts together, moving my head from side to side every few minutes as I nibbled, sucked, and squeezed until her nipples were distended and red.

I moved slowly down her body, licking along the bottom of her rib cage, and trailing kisses down the soft swell of her belly. When I got to her hips I bypassed her pussy, instead kissing my way down one leg and up the other. When I reached her inner thigh I pulled the soft skin between my teeth, biting down and sucking, marking her and then licking the spot to soothe the skin. When I lifted my head, I could clearly see a lovely red hickey. It was probably ridiculous of me, but it gave me a sense of primal satisfaction to know that I'd marked her as mine.

I paused. Mine? I rolled the word around in my head, recognizing that it felt right. Elana was mine, whether she knew it or not.

I turned my attention to her pussy.

"You're bare?" I asked unnecessarily.

"I hate hair down there," she answered distractedly. "It feels itchy."

"I like it."

The minute my tongue brushed the outside of her pussy, Elana jackknifed up with a gasp. I clamped my hands on her hips, holding her down, and settled myself on my stomach between her open legs. I explored every centimeter of her beautiful pussy, flattening my tongue and licking up her essence until she was begging me.

"Please Toya, I need to come."

I looked up to see that she was thrashing her head from side to side, her fingers clenching the comforter so tightly her skin almost looked translucent.

"I got you, baby girl."

I slid my tongue into her channel as far as it would reach, sliding it in and out, fucking her with my tongue while Elana lifted her hips up to meet me. She was already drenched, and I knew she was close. Releasing her hips, I reached one hand up to pinch her nipple at the same time that I rolled her clit between my fingers.

Elana screeched as her orgasm hit.

"Fuuuck!"

She shuddered and shook beneath me, thrashing so hard I wondered if she was going to throw me right off her. She was much smaller than I was, but she was surprisingly strong.

I slowed my motions as the aftershocks trembled through her. When she sagged into the bed I pulled away, licking my lips to taste her essence one more time. Elana lay on the bed, eyes screwed shut as she tried to catch her breath. I took a moment to watch the slight jiggle of her breasts as she breathed.

I shifted myself to her side, pulling the bottom of the comforter up around her before sliding next to her. I turned until I could throw my arm over her stomach and laid my head down on her chest. I could hear her heartbeat gradually slowing.

After a bit she must have opened her eyes because I could feel her watching me. I shifted my head, resting my chin just above her right breast, and met her gaze. I studied her, trying to determine how she was feeling. Her expression looked like a mixture of happiness and confusion.

"About the deal we had for you to be my fake girlfriend?" I started.

"What about it?"

"I want to renegotiate."

I saw a flash of unease cross her face.

"Renegotiate how?" she asked carefully.

I wondered what that was about. Did she not understand how incredible this was? Whatever was happening between us, she had to be feeling it too.

"I don't want you to be my fake girlfriend anymore."

Elana searched my face. "Okay..."

"I want you to be my real girlfriend."

Her eyes lit up and she gave me a hopeful smile. "Really?"

"Yeah, really. Also, we need to do that about a million times more."

She slid her arm around me to hug me closer to her.

"I guess we could do that," she said saucily. "But first I'm going to need some recovery time."

"This whole thing has hit me by surprise," I continued. "It's like I'm just seeing you for the first time and I can't believe I missed you all this time."

"It's because you had me in the friend zone since the day we met."

I nodded against her chest. "Yeah, I guess I did. But you're not there now, baby."

She studied me for a long moment, then whispered so softly that I almost didn't catch it.

"Please don't hurt me."

I leaned down and pressed my lips against her sternum. "I won't. I promise."

That night we slept snuggled together from the start, our legs tangled, our heads close together. At some point Elana must have gotten up because I felt the bed shift under her weight as she crawled back under the covers. I opened one eye, squinting at the sunshine coming in through the windows.

"What time is it?" I asked, my voice raspy.

"Just after seven."

Elana pulled the blanket off of me, revealing my naked body. I stretched like a cat under her perusal, subtly widening the space between my legs. Without a word, she leaned down to lick my pussy, and I damn near levitated off the bed as instant arousal hit me in a wave. I groaned and grabbed her head, stopping her motions.

"What's wrong?" she asked, looking like a kid who lost their favorite toy.

"I have a better idea," I said. "Switch directions."

"Huh?"

I gave her an indulgent smile. "Get that sweet pussy up here so I can get you off at the same time."

Her eyes brightened with understanding.

"Sixty-nine? I like how you think."

Elana

After we'd brought each other to orgasm, we ordered breakfast from room service, sitting on the little balcony outside our room and eating in the warm sunshine.

"This bacon is perfect," Toya said happily as she waved a piece in her hand. "It's crispy but not burned."

I smiled. "My waffles are good too."

I paused, then added, "Hey, can I ask you a question?"

"Sure."

"You told me that when your mom asked about your girlfriend that I was the first person who popped in your head?"

She nodded.

"Why?"

She looked at me thoughtfully.

"You know, I don't really know. She asked about it and I was kind of scrambling and I guess I thought, well if someone I know would be my girlfriend, who would it be? And then I saw your face in my mind. Why do you ask?"

I took another bite of waffle to give me some time.

"I have a confession."

She raised one eyebrow as she chewed on another piece of bacon. Good lord, Toya could even make eating bacon look sexy.

"I've always liked you as more than a friend. In fact, I had a crush on you for a long time."

She dropped her bacon onto her plate in surprise. "You did?"

I nodded. "Yeah, ever since the first day we met."

"Why didn't you say something?"

"I didn't want things to get awkward between us," I confessed. "You weren't giving me any hint that you liked me that way, so I didn't think you'd reciprocate."

She looked thoughtful. "Yeah, that's probably right. I think I was subconsciously attracted to you for a while, and that's why your name popped out of my mouth with my mom. But I wasn't getting any kind of romantic vibes between us until we went on this trip."

"Well in that case, I'm glad I agreed to be your fake girlfriend."

"Me too."

Toya's phone dinged and she rolled her eyes as she picked it up to return the text. "Mom wants to know if I'm awake. It's nine in the morning, and I'm an adult, but she doesn't think I know how to set a damn alarm."

Her thumbs flew as she typed out a response.

"I guess we should start getting ready," she said. "I'm supposed to join Tina and the rest of the bridesmaids to get my hair and make-up done."

I stayed on the balcony staring out at the mountains and finishing my breakfast while Toya showered and changed clothes. She popped out a while later, wearing her maid of honor dress.

"How do I look?" she asked, twirling. The fabric rose around her legs as she turned.

"Wow. You look beautiful."

Her dress was a dusty pink satin number that draped down to her calves. It had bands of material that laid across the top of her arms, leaving her shoulders bare, and a tastefully low-cut front. The waist was cinched in matching fabric. She'd paired the dress with black high heeled shoes.

"Now you're even taller than me," I grumbled, pointing at her shoes.

She leaned down to give me a fast kiss. "I like you just the way you are, baby. We fit together just right."

After Toya left with a promise to see me at the ceremony, I took a long, hot bath. I leaned back against the side, submerging myself up to my neck, and replayed the previous day's events in my head. I had no idea when I got up yesterday morning that my relationship with Toya would change so dramatically.

Not that I was complaining of course. When she told me that she wanted to renegotiate our relationship status, I almost died. For six long months I'd waited for Toya to notice me. Now that she had, I wondered what would happen when we went home to Seattle. Telling myself that we'd work it out, I puttered around the room for a while before putting on the off-white suit that I'd brought for the wedding. I paired it with a pale pink shirt and a pair of dark pink mules with a two-inch heel. Pulling my hair back into a ponytail, I studied myself in the mirror. I looked good. Happy.

As I headed down to the wedding, I just hoped it would last. I'd had a lot of bad luck with relationships, especially with the last woman I dated. Rebecca was a total psycho and in retrospect, I was glad it had taken a while for things to happen between me and Toya. I probably needed the time to recover as much as Toya did.

The rest of the day passed pretty quickly. Tina and Damon's wedding was pretty short, less than an hour. Tina was a beautiful bride, but I couldn't take my eyes off her sister. Toya looked incredibly happy for her sister, beaming at her throughout the ceremony. As she walked down the aisle on the best man's arm after the ceremony, her eyes found mine. She sent me a wink that made goose bumps rise on my skin.

The bridal party and immediate family was pulled away to take pictures, so I decided to use the break between the ceremony to go back to the room and read for a while. My e-reader was always jam packed with books, and as much as I enjoyed being with Toya, it was nice to relax and get some quiet time. I was in introvert at heart, and I needed some time to recharge before I had to "people" at the reception.

By the time I came back downstairs, the reception was in full swing. I wandered around until I found Toya, then slid my arm around her waist. She did the same, leaning down to give me a quick peck on the cheek.

"Hi baby."

"Hi yourself," I responded. "You looked so beautiful up there, you totally outshined the bride."

"Hey now!" I turned to see Tina and Damon coming up behind us.

"No one's more beautiful than my bride," Damon told me with a wink.

I laughed. "I apologize. You're right. Toya is an old hag next to Tina."

"That's right," Tina responded as we all laughed.

The wedding coordinator alerted us that it was time for dinner. I sat at the bridal party table, squeezed in between Toya and her mother. We all chatted easily as we enjoyed dinner, then the toasts started. The best man went first, and then Toya.

She took the microphone and glanced around the crowd before turning her gaze to her sister and new brother-in-law.

"My name is Toya, and I have the pleasure of being Tina's big sister as well as the maid of honor. I gotta tell you, I never really believed in love. It felt like something in a fairy tale, not something that happened in real life. Until I saw my sister with Damon. The love that they share is pure and beautiful and it's been an inspiration to me."

She turned her gaze towards me. "Seeing that love was real helped me recognize it when it finally came into my own life."

She paused for a moment, and we stared into each other's eyes until someone cleared their throat. Visibly shaking herself, she turned back to Tina and Damon and resumed her toast.

"Tina, Damon, I wish you health, happiness, and lots of great sexy times."

Next to me, Mrs. Hamilton groaned.

"I love you both. Cheers."

Everyone lifted their glasses and drank as Toya returned to her seat. Her hand immediately found mine, and impulsively I turned to kiss her cheek. Toya turned, and our lips met instead. Our kiss was sweet. A promise for the future. And I'd never been happier.

Toya

Two weeks later...

I rushed into the restaurant late. I'd gotten caught up at work, and the whole group was already there. Sliding into the chair next to Elana, I squeezed her hand under the table and greeted our friends.

The last two weeks had been incredible. We'd been engaging in non-stop sex, together every minute we weren't working. When we weren't bringing each other pleasure, we spent time together and did typical couple things like cooking, reading, watching movies, and hiking. I'd never fallen into a relationship so easily like I had with Elana. There was no drama between us like I'd had in other relationships.

Not a day went by that I didn't chastise myself for not noticing her sooner. How was it that we hung out together for six months and I'd never given more than a passing thought to how attractive she was? Maybe I'd been more distraught over my last break-up than I thought I'd been. The trip to Bend for the wedding had taken the blinders off, that's for sure. Elana was the woman I'd been waiting for my whole life.

"Ladies, I have an announcement."

I spoke loudly to be heard over my friends' chatter. They all turned to look at me curiously. I looked at Elana, who nodded to let me know she was still on board with my sharing the news. I lifted our joined hands to rest on top of the table for all to see.

"Elana and I are seeing each other."

The table erupted.

"Finally! I knew you two liked each other," Jewel said.

She shot a look at her partner, Alice. "I told you, didn't I?"

Alice nodded. "You did."

"What the hell took you so long?" This was from our friend Miranda. "We thought you'd never hook up."

"It's more than hooking up," I clarified.

"They're in love....," Jennifer sang out.

I rolled my eyes.

"Well, now you all know," I said. "We don't need to make a big deal out of it."

"Okay everyone, time to pay up," Elizabeth announced as she took a twenty out of her wallet. "Who had this month in the pool?"

"What pool?" Elana asked in confusion.

"We had a pool going on which month you two dummies would finally realize you were crazy about each other and start dating," Jewel explained. "And I had July, so thank you everyone for your bets. You may pay me now."

Elana and I shared bemused looks as the rest of the table all threw twenties at Jewel. I had to ask...

"Wait a minute, you all knew we liked each other before we did?"

"It was so obvious," Alice piped up. "Elana would get all red and twittery when you were around, and you were trying way too hard to ignore her. Besides, we know you both pretty well, and it was obvious that you were perfect for each other."

"That's not true," I protested. "We've been friends ever since we met but I didn't like her back then, not romantically anyway. I wasn't trying to ignore her."

"Did you ever do anything alone before you went to Bend for the wedding?" Jewel asked.

"No."

"Yet you've hung out with everyone else in the group," she pointed out. "It was totally obvious you were avoiding your feelings."

"It wasn't obvious to me," I grumbled. "I don't know why the hell you all didn't tell us then, it would have saved us a lot of lost time."

Jewel rolled her eyes as she gathered up her winnings. "And miss watching you two stumble around before you realized? No way we'd miss that."

I sighed and lowered my head to rest on Elana's shoulder as I tried to remember acting differently towards Elana before she became my fake girlfriend but drew a blank.

"I'm glad we're here for your amusement."

"We're happy for you two, truly," Alice said.

"And so are Lila and Christine," Miranda announced, referring to our friend and her rock star girlfriend/boss. She held up her phone, obviously texting with our other friends.

"Wow, the lesbian gossip network works fast," I said wryly.

Someone changed the subject, and the rest of the dinner went by quickly. I'd been pretty sure that our friends would be happy to hear we were dating, but it was nice to know for sure. Maybe it was inevitable that the two single women in the group would get together.

As we left the restaurant, I squeezed Elana's hand.

"Your place or mine?"

"Mine. I got a delivery today I think you'll like."

I raised my eyebrows.

"Well, that's intriguing."

Elana just gave me a smile. We walked hand in hand to her apartment, which was about a mile from the restaurant. It was a nice night and it felt good to walk after eating such a large meal. Elana rented a townhouse on a quiet residential street. As we walked up the street, we noticed someone sitting on her stairs.

"What the—?"

Elana stiffened, pulling her hand away from mine. I looked at her curiously. Her mouth was open in surprise.

A tall, blonde, Barbie doll looking white woman pushed herself off the stairs and ran to Elana, throwing her arms around her and pressing her lips against my girlfriend's.

"Elana! I've missed you so much!"

Elana

I pushed Rebecca off me, my skin crawling. My mind was racing. How had she found me after all this time? I felt sick to my stomach.

"Who's this, Elana?" Toya asked. Her voice sounded cold and accusatory.

"No one," I said.

"I'm her girlfriend," Rebecca said at the same time. She remained standing next to me, closer than the restraining order allowed. I resisted the urge to shove her farther away from me, knowing from experience that it would ramp her up even more.

"No, you're not."

"Yes, I am," she said in her little girl voice that always grated on my nerves. "Did you miss me while I was away on my trip, love?"

It was weird how she made it sound like she was on vacation instead of in jail and later the mental hospital. Rebecca gripped my arm, her long fake fingernails digging into my skin, and laid her head on my shoulder.

"You're not cheating on me with this...this person, are you Elana? You know how I feel about you cheating on me when I'm not around. You've been a very bad girl."

Her baby talk voice grated on me. Ignoring the crazy lady, I turned to my actual girlfriend.

"Toya, I can explain. This isn't what it looks like."

Toya's expression was a mixture of shock, hurt, and rage.

"I don't need to hear your excuses," she said coldly.

"But..."

I pulled away from Rebecca, reaching out to touch Toya's arm, but she threw up her hand, holding her palm out only inches from my face.

"I'm done. You know how I feel about cheaters."

"I'm not..."

"Save it," she bit out. "I can't believe you would do this to me. I can't believe I fell for your act. We're done. Don't call me or contact me again."

I could feel my heart breaking as she stalked away without another word. What the hell? Did she trust me so little? She wouldn't even give me a chance to explain what was happening. I could feel my temper rising. How dare she treat me like that?

"Don't worry Lainie, Rebecca's here now," my ex simpered. "The important thing is that we're together again after so long."

I turned to face the woman who had stalked me for over a year before I got a restraining order against her and moved to another state. I was so furious my vision was tinted with red.

Rebecca and I had dated for a while when I lived in Oregon. After four dates, I realized that it wasn't going to work. The trouble began after I broke up with her. She told me she was in love with me and started calling and texting me incessantly, showing up at my home and my work, and acting more and more obsessed with me. I tried moving apartments and blocking her number, but she kept coming for me, thick in her delusion that we were still together. Calls, texts, increasingly creepy gifts left on my doorstep, it all became too much.

Then the threats started. I hoped she'd get tired and move on, but she didn't. The day she broke into my apartment and trashed everything was the day I got the police involved. If I closed my eyes, I could still see the chilling message she'd left on my living room wall with lipstick.

"You'll never escape me. We belong together."

I filed a restraining order, and after she violated it twice the police finally arrested her. In jail they determined that she was mentally ill and took her to a facility for treatment. It seemed like a good outcome, and I felt pretty confident that I wouldn't see her again. But just in case, I'd found a job in Seattle and moved as an extra layer of protection. I'd closed all my social media accounts and warned friends and family not to talk to Rebecca if she contacted them.

"How did you find me?" I demanded. "The last I heard the state had you on a psych hold."

Rebecca gave me a coquettish smile. "I have my ways."

I pressed the emergency call button on my phone, ringing 911.

"911, what's your emergency?"

"Someone has violated a restraining order. I need the police."

"Oh, come on Lainie, don't be like that," Rebecca whined.

I ignored her, giving the dispatcher my address. They assured me that there was a cruiser a few blocks away that would be there in a few minutes, so I resolved to keep Rebecca talking so they could pick her up. I hung up on the dispatcher and turned to Rebecca with a forced smile.

"They can't come right now," I lied.

Rebecca relaxed and moved closer to me. Meanwhile, my mind was racing. I honestly never expected to see her again. I had no idea how she'd found me here, but I hoped that this time she'd get the help she needed, far away from me. There was no way I wanted to go back to never knowing when she would show up and what she would do.

"So, how have you been?" I asked. "You look good."

Actually, she looked like that little white girl on the dancing show with the mean teacher. Her face was pale, and her blonde hair was pulled up in a high ponytail that was so tight I was surprised she didn't get a headache from it.

Rebecca perked up. That was the thing about her, her moods switched rapidly, especially if flattery was involved.

"I'm fine Elana, now that I found you. It was hard to track you down but now we can finally be together again."

I kept her talking until the cops came. Rebecca didn't make any effort to escape, likely because in her mind we were still together, and she'd done nothing wrong. After verifying both of our identities and the restraining order status, they took a report from me. I breathed a sigh of relief as they put Rebecca in the back of the cop car and drove her away from me. Hopefully for the last time. She waved to me from the back window with a big smile, presumably thinking that she would be back soon. I shivered in revulsion.

As I returned to my apartment, I saw the box that I'd left on the dining room table. It was a new vibrator for me and Toya to play with. I swept the box into the trash with a growl of frustration. I didn't need it anymore.

Then I threw myself on the couch and finally let myself cry.

I thought things were good with me and Toya, but if she didn't trust me, we couldn't go further. I wasn't going to beg for her to talk to me and let me explain. She'd had her chance. She was done with me? Okay, well, I was done with her too. Maybe Rebecca had done me a favor showing me Toya's true colors. I didn't want to be in a relationship with someone who didn't trust me. That was a hard line for me.

Toya

"You're an idiot."

I looked up from my phone to see Miranda leaning against my SUV. I'd just gotten off work and I was dirty and tired. The last thing I expected was to see my friend loitering in the parking lot of my work.

"What are you doing here Miranda?"

"You haven't been responding to anyone's messages all week."

I sighed. It had been five days since I discovered Elana's deception, and it had been all I could do to just go to work. I didn't have the energy for things like eating, sleeping, or responding to nosy texts from my friends. I just went to work and then sat on the couch staring into space. It was all I could handle right now.

"I've been busy." I lied.

Miranda raised one eyebrow, giving me the "don't bullshit" look she'd perfected over the years as a social worker working with runaway youth and street kids.

"You broke Elana's heart, you know."

Her voice conveyed disappointment with me, and I reared back.

"I broke *her* heart? I think you mean she broke *mine*."

"You didn't even give her a chance to explain what was going on," she chided.

"I think the busty blonde hanging all over her was all the explanation I needed."

Miranda huffed in annoyance.

"You know, me and Elana clicked right away, because we're both from Oregon. We spent a lot of time together, and I got to know her pretty well, to hear her story."

"So?"

"So...do you know why she moved to Seattle?"

I shrugged. We'd talked about a lot of things over the last few weeks, but somehow that topic never came up.

"I don't really care."

"Well, you should care Toya, because the reason she moved up here was to get away from a stalker who kept threatening her. The crazy woman scratched up her car and broke into her apartment and trashed everything Elana owned."

I felt a pinch in my chest thinking that Elana had a stalker, but ruthlessly shoved it away. Having a stalker didn't excuse what she did. Miranda shoved a piece of paper at me.

"What's this?" I asked.

"A copy of the restraining order that I pulled off the state criminal database."

Since Miranda worked with runaway youth, she had access to a lot of information.

"Her stalker, Rebecca, was who you saw at her house. Elana had been hiding in Seattle, but Rebecca somehow found her here."

"What?" I asked in shock.

"This woman terrorized Elana for almost a year, and then she shows up in violation of the restraining order and what do you do? You leave your girlfriend alone with a crazy person, accuse her of cheating on you, and break up with her."

Miranda gave me a glare that could melt steel. "And that's why you're an idiot. I expected better from you, Toya. We all did."

I looked down at the restraining order, scanning the recitation of all the things Rebecca had done to terrorize Elana, including breaking into her house, destroying her belongings, and leaving increasingly threatening messages. I pressed my hand against my stomach, suddenly feeling like I would throw up. How could I have been so wrong?

I must have said that part out loud, because Miranda answered, "You could be so wrong because you let your past relationship overshadow what you know about Elana. You didn't give her a chance. The minute there was an issue, you just ran away and left her in a potentially dangerous situation. She could have gotten hurt."

"Oh my God, I fucked up."

My legs buckled, and I sat my ass down on the ground near my car.

"Yeah, you did. The question is, do you love her?"

"Of course I do."

I realized it was true, although I'd never admitted it to anyone, even myself. That's why it hurt so bad when I thought she'd betrayed me. I loved Elana, and my heart said she loved me too, yet I'd ignored all that when the blonde Barbie doll showed up, sure that I'd picked another cheater to date.

"What are you going to do about it?" Miranda demanded.

"I don't know."

"You better fix this Toya. Because if I have to choose, I'm telling you right now I'm choosing Elana. She's the wronged party here."

I gripped my head in my hands. "What am I going to do? I fucked up so bad. I really miss her."

"You better start groveling, my friend, and pray that she forgives you."

I pushed myself up to standing. "I'm going over there now."

Miranda patted my arm. "That's my girl. Good luck."

I got into my car and raced over to Elana's house. I had no idea what I was going to say, but I hoped inspiration would strike when I got there. If I ever found a parking spot. Elana lived in a neighborhood with lots of shops and restaurants and it took me a good twenty minutes to find a spot to park my car. Even still, I was drawing a blank on how to make this right.

I walked back to her place from my spot several blocks away, walking as fast as I could. By the time I got there, I was sweaty and out of breath. I ran up her steps and knocked on the door. When Elana didn't answer, I pounded on the door and called her name.

"Elana!!!"

"What?"

I started as I heard her voice from behind me. Elana was on the top step, a cloth grocery bag full of food in one hand, her keys in the other. She looked exhausted and so beautiful that it made my heart hurt.

"Elana."

"What do you want, Toya?" she asked in a defeated tone.

"Can we talk? Please?"

"I think you've said enough to me," she said, pushing past me to unlock her door. "Goodbye."

"Wait!"

I shoved my foot in the door to keep her from closing it. I was glad I was wearing steel-toed boots as she slammed the door against my foot with freakish strength for such a little thing.

Elana made a growling noise and stalked into the kitchen to put away the groceries. I followed her in, standing by the island that separated the kitchen from the living room. I watched as she put the groceries away, slamming doors, and when she finished she turned to face me, fists on her hips.

"Well?" she snapped, raising one eyebrow. "What's so important that you barged in on me after you said very clearly that you didn't want to talk to me ever again?"

"I was an asshole."

"Yeah, no kidding. Thanks for stopping by. Bye now."

I held out my hands in supplication.

"I didn't realize...I didn't know about the stalker thing until Miranda told me."

"Oh, so if Miranda says it, it's true, but your girlfriend you don't want to hear from or believe."

"I'm really sorry Elana. I overreacted. When I saw that girl I had a flashback to what happened to me before, and I got jealous and angry and...I shouldn't have treated you like that. I feel terrible about what happened. I know I fucked up."

Elana's face was fierce and angry. She looked so hurt that I wanted to kick my own ass.

"You know what Toya? I already had one unhealthy relationship, I don't want another."

I nodded. "If you give me another chance, I'll make it up to you. You have my word, nothing like that will ever happen again."

When Elana continued to stare at me I added, "I love you."

She threw up her hands and stalked away into the living room. "You think that's supposed to fix everything?"

I followed her.

"No, but I want you to know where I stand."

She flopped onto the couch with a deep sigh. "Great."

I sat on the coffee table next to her and took her hand in mine, praying she wouldn't punch me.

"I know I was wrong, and if something had happened to you because I left you with that lunatic, I would have never forgiven myself," I began. "I let my history get in the way of us, what I know to be true about you. I know you would never betray me Elana, I just...well, I think between telling our friends and realizing that I loved you, it kind of freaked me out a little bit, and that made a small part of me look for a reason to run."

Elana's gaze softened and I knew I was getting through to her.

"I've waited my whole life for a woman like you," I continued. "I love you like I've never loved anyone before in my life. I'm so damn sorry I hurt you. You're a gift, and I promise I'll spend the rest of my life showing you how much you mean to me. I'll never doubt you again. I'll do anything to prove to you how much I love you."

"Anything?" she asked, her expression softening.

"Yes, name it."

"Could you take a shower? No offense but you smell like wood chips, insulation, and sweat."

I laughed for the first time in a week.

"Yeah, it got pretty hot in the house we're remodeling, and then I parked a million blocks away because there were no spots by your house. I guess I should've gone home to clean up first, but I didn't want to be apart from you for another minute."

She nodded, her face turning tender. I lifted her hand to my mouth and kissed her knuckles.

"Please. Will you give me another chance?"

Elana met my gaze. "If something like this happens again, we're done. There will be no more second chances. I have too much self-respect to let someone treat me like that."

"I understand."

"Okay then, you'd better clean up. You're buying me a nice dinner tonight to make up for being a jealous asshole."

"You got it, baby."

"Oh, and by the way, I love you too. Although I've been wondering why for the past several days."

I pulled her up to standing and kissed her softly on the lips. All was right in my world now. And I'd do my damnedest to make sure it stayed that way.

Epilogue – Elana

One year later...

"I'm glad we came back here."

I leaned against Toya as we sat in the hot tub on the deck of one of the private cabins at Great Bend Resort. We'd returned to the place where we first fell in love, but this time we were here for a different wedding – our own.

I glanced at my wife's left hand, seeing the plain gold band that glistened on her ring finger. Toya wanted something she could wear at work, and anything with a stone might get caught in the equipment. I wore a matching band on my hand, along with the small and tasteful diamond engagement ring Toya gave me when she proposed.

We'd moved in together about a month after our big break-up, and four months later, Toya had proposed to me at Christmas dinner with her family. Honestly, I don't know who was more excited about the proposal: me or her mom.

"Your mom was so cute today," I told Toya. "That speech she gave at the wedding was incredible."

"It was," Toya agreed. "I'm pretty sure she likes you better than me now. So, how's it feel to be a married woman?"

"Pretty good," I responded.

"Only pretty good?"

"Well, we haven't consummated the marriage yet. I'll have to reserve judgement until I see how that goes."

Toya laughed. The one thing we never struggled with was the physical part of our relationship, although honestly, after what happened when Rebecca showed up, any little disagreement we had felt pretty minor. We'd both worked hard on keeping good communication between us.

My wife stepped out of the hot tub, holding her hand out.

"What's happening?" I asked.

"I'm going to consummate the hell out of this marriage," she said. "I plan to make you come over and over again until you pass out."

I took her hand and stepped out of the hot tub. Since our space was private, we were both totally naked. I wasn't going to complain about that. I loved my wife's body as much as I knew she loved mine.

"I approve of that plan. And by the way, I have a present for you, wife."

"A present? What is it?" Toya said excitedly.

She followed me into the suite, and I dug around in my suitcase until I found the new vibrator I'd purchased for this occasion. I figured a honeymoon called for new sex toys. I didn't want things to get stale in the bedroom. I pressed the button, activating the toy, and Toya's eyes widened.

"What are you going to do with that?" she asked saucily.

"How about you get on the bed, and I'll show you?"

She stepped closer and kissed me softly.

"I love you."

"You'll love me more after we use this," I teased. "I bought it at that sex toy party that Miranda had while you were out of town last month."

"Damn, I'm sorry I missed that."

Toya had been out of town meeting her new nephew when the party happened. He was an adorable little guy who screamed his way through our ceremony until Damon took him outside.

Tina had been the maid of honor for Toya, while Jewel had been mine.

I pressed the button on our new toy and a loud vibrating sound filled the room. Toya eagerly hopped on the bed, crooking her finger at me.

"Come on Elana, let's break that baby in."

I took a leap and landed on the bed next to her, then rolled on top of her. My mouth found hers, and I kissed her deeply, exploring the recesses of her mouth.

"Ready to have old married people sex?" I asked with a mischievous smile when we finally broke apart, breathless.

Toya nodded. "With you? Always."

***

If you liked this book, please consider leaving a review or rating on my author page to let me know.

Want a free book? Join my newsletter and receive a copy of my book "Hotel Spanking" for free. My newsletter subscribers are the first to hear about all of my new releases and sales. Click here[1] and download your free book today.

Be sure to keep reading for a free preview from Reba Bale's "Divorce Recovery" series, available now on all major retailers.

---

1.   *https://bit.ly/rebabooks*

Special Preview

Spanking Justice: A Middle-Aged Divorcee's First Spanking
The Divorce Recovery Team Series
Book 1
By Reba Bale

"Congratulations Amy, you're officially divorced."

Mark Winston, her divorce attorney, slid the folder of papers across the heavy wooden desk. Amy leaned forward hesitantly and placed her hand on the folder without picking it up. She could still see a faint tan line where her wedding ring used to be.

She bit her lip and sighed. "Thanks. I guess."

"What is it?" Mark asked, his deep voice causing a shiver down her spine. "Most people are relieved when the process is finally completed. You're free to move forward with your life now, like your ex-husband will do."

Amy nodded. "I know. I hope that feeling of relief will come later. It's just..."

"Just what?" Mark asked, tipping his head to the side curiously.

Amy studied him for a moment. He really was a handsome man. She estimated his age to be early fifties, about ten years older than she was. She had turned forty a few months ago. His hair was dark and thick, with silver highlights near his temples giving him a distinguished air. Small lines bracketed his mouth as he gave her a small encouraging smile. Something about him made her feel comfortable to confide in him.

"I can't help but think about all the things I did wrong in the relationship," she said, her voice small. "If I knew now what I know then, would I have done some things differently to save the relationship."

Mark looked at her intently. "You gave almost twenty years to your marriage Amy. You put your own career on the back burner to raise your son. You kept the house. And then your husband decided to move on to someone younger. It's a pretty typical story, honestly."

"I know," she nodded. "But I've been thinking of all the times I nagged, all the times I was too tired from running around with my son to take care of myself, all the times I said no to sex or date night. John cheated and there's absolutely no excuse for that. But I realize at some point I gave up on the marriage too. I'm having a hard time forgiving myself for the things I did, or didn't do, to keep the relationship alive."

Mark looked at her thoughtfully. "You'll need to forgive yourself in order to move on," he said. "Otherwise, you'll just stagnate and think about the past. You do want to move on, don't you?"

Amy nodded again. "Yes, of course. I just need to stop beating myself up."

Mark steepled his hands on the desk and stared at her intently until she met his gaze for the first time since she walked into the office. His eyes were serious. "What if I told you that we have a way to help you move on? A service that has helped so many women like yourselves recover from their divorces and go on to have a happy life."

She looked at him curiously. "How? What do you mean?"

"Our firm offers a unique service for people like you. People who want to, shall we say, accept the consequences of their own part in the demise of their marriage. We will punish you for your actions, then you can move on. We give you absolution of a sorts. Then you are able to forgive yourself too."

"Punish me? Like what, a spanking?" she laughed, ignoring the small thrill in her belly when she said it.

Mark's eyes sparked as if he knew what she was thinking. "Yes, that's exactly right. We call it our Divorce Discipline package. You agree to be spanked or punished by us for everything you did wrong, then it's over and you can move on."

"You're offering to spank me?" she squeaked.

"That's exactly what I'm offering you. It's safe, confidential, and quite therapeutic," he said, pulling an envelope out of his drawer.

"I know it's a lot to think about so take some time. Here's the contract for our Divorce Discipline package. Read it over, and if you decide you want to move forward, call my assistant, and tell her you want a DD appointment with me after hours. I'll handle your case myself."

"Is this a joke?" she asked, looking around for a hidden camera.

For more of the story, check out "Spanking Justice" by Reba Bale, available for immediate download on your favorite retail sites today.

***

Want a free book? Join my newsletter and receive a free copy of my book "Hotel Spanking" for free. I promise I will only email you when there are new releases or special sales, so go to https://www.bit.ly/rebabooks to sign up today.

Other Books by Reba Bale

Check out my other books, available on most major online retailers now:

Friends to Lovers Series

The Divorcee's First Time: A Lesbian Romance

My BFF's Sister

My Rockstar Assistant

My College Crush

My Secret Crush

My Fake Girlfriend

My Holiday Love

My Valentine's Gift

Unlikely Doms Series

Alpha in a Sweater Vest

Alpha Plumber

Hotel Spanking

Alpha Student

Alpha Yogi

The Voyeur Romance Series

Naughty Sunbathing

Naughty Dinner Date

Naughty Laundry Date

Naughty Camping

The Spanking Therapy Series

The Reluctant Bride's First Spanking

The Reluctant Bride Gets Caught

The Billionaire Gets Punished

The Divorce Recovery Series

Spanking Justice: A Middle-Aged Divorcee's First Spanking
A Punishing Workout: Spanked by the Trainer
A Disciplined Budget: Spanked by the Accountant
The Curvy Reporter Gets Punished

Paying for Tuition

The Babysitter's Ride Home
The Babysitter's First Menage
The Teaching Assistant's Lesson
The Billionaire's Assistant

The Marriage Survival Series

Finding His Alpha: A Wife's First Spanking
Watching His Wife: The First Time Sharing
Exploring His Fantasy: A First Time Gay Ménage

Toys for Grown-Ups Series

Financial Punishment
Menage a Geek

Punishing Holidays

Turkey and a Spanking
Shopping and a Spanking

Standalones:

Share Me: A Cheating Husband's Punishment
Tornado Warning
Summer in Paradise
The Ride of My Life
Taken by Surprise
Hotwife in the Woods
Hotwife on the Beach

Want a free book? Join my newsletter and receive a free copy of my book "Hotel Spanking" for free. I promise I will only email you when there are new releases or special sales, so got to https://www.bit.ly/rebabooks and sign up today.

About the Author

Reba Bale loves writing naughty stories where the characters are able to tap into their inner fantasies and experience spanking, bondage, humiliation, or other activities on the non-vanilla side of life. When Reba is not writing she is reading the same naughty stories she likes to write.

Be sure to follow Reba on your favorite retailer and sign up for her newsletter so you are first to hear about all the new releases. Sign up at https://www.bit.ly/rebabooks.

Don't miss out!

Visit the website below and you can sign up to receive emails whenever Reba Bale publishes a new book. There's no charge and no obligation.

https://books2read.com/r/B-A-IDTM-ZJEZB

BOOKS 2 READ

Connecting independent readers to independent writers.

Did you love *My Fake Girlfriend*? Then you should read *The Divorcee's First Time: A Hot Friends-to-Lovers Lesbian Romance*[1] by Reba Bale!

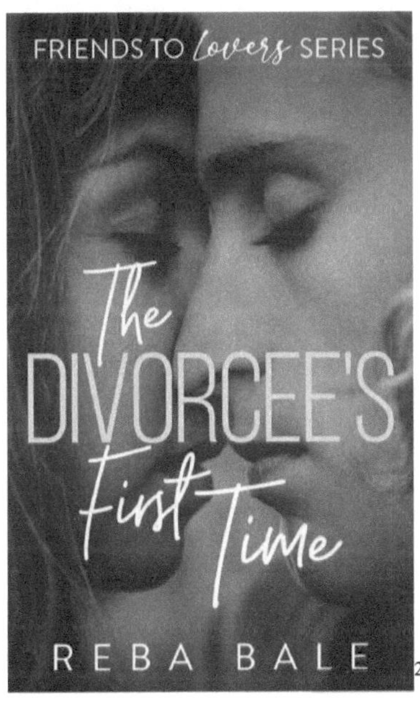

[2]

When Jennifer goes out with her best friend Susan to celebrate her divorce, she gets more than she bargained for. The dominant older woman gives Jennifer her first time lesbian experience and changes things forever. Will it be a one-time thing, or will their hot and steamy night lead to more? This friends to lovers novella is standalone romance intended for adult audiences only, due to explicit scenes and light BDSM.

---

1. https://books2read.com/u/bpznKX

2. https://books2read.com/u/bpznKX